THIS WALKER BOOK BELONGS TO:

Ch

ChLoeY

For Gemma

First published 1988 by Walker Books Ltd
87 Vauxhall Walk, London SE11 5HJ

This edition published 1997

4 6 8 10 9 7 5

Text and illustrations © 1988 Chris Riddell

This book has been typeset in Veronan Light Educational.

Printed in Hong Kong/China

British Library Cataloguing in Publication Data
A catalogue record for this book is
available from the British Library.

ISBN 0-7445-5447-0

THE
TROUBLE WITH
ELEPHANTS

Written and illustrated by
CHRIS RIDDELL

WALKER BOOKS
AND SUBSIDIARIES
LONDON • BOSTON • SYDNEY

The trouble with elephants is . . .

they spill the bath water
when they get in . . .

and they leave a pink elephant
ring when they get out.

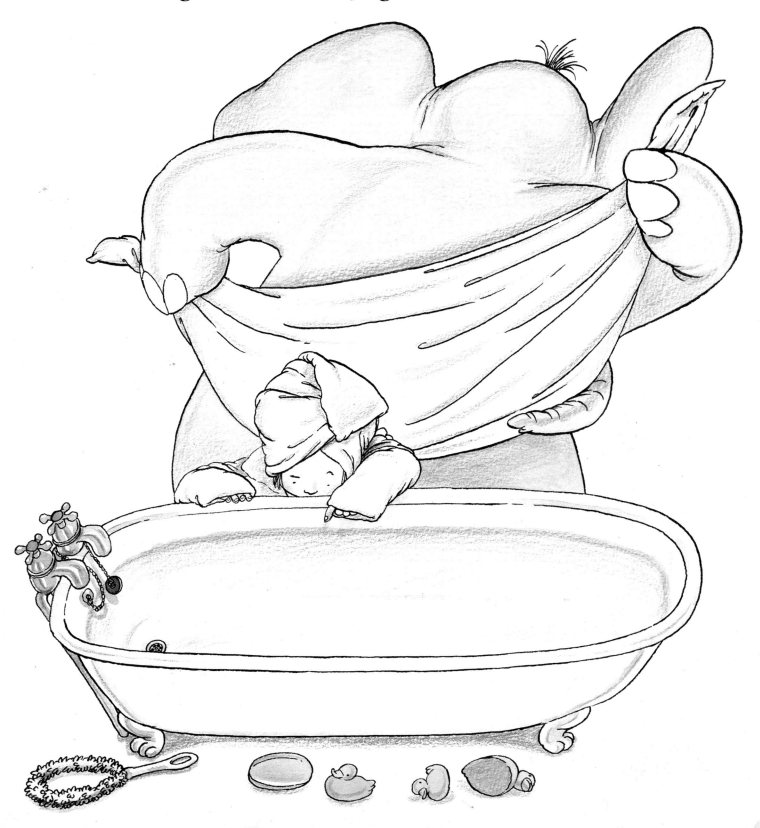

They take all the bedclothes and they snore elephant snores which rattle the window panes.

The only way to wake a sleeping
elephant is to shout "Mouse!"
in its ear.

Then it will slide down the
bannisters to breakfast.

Elephants travel four in a car – two in the front and two in the back.

You can always tell when an elephant
is visiting because there'll be a car
outside with three elephants in it.

Sometimes elephants ride bicycles . . .

but not very often.

The trouble with elephants is that on elephant picnics they eat all the buns before you've finished your first one.

Elephants drink their lemonade through their trunks, and if you're not looking, they drink yours too.

On elephant picnics they play games
like leap-elephant and skipping,
which they're good at.

And sometimes they play hide and seek, which they're not very good at.

The trouble with elephants is . . .

well, there are all sorts of troubles . . .

all sorts of troubles . . .

but the real trouble is . . .

you can't help but love them.

MORE WALKER PAPERBACKS
For You to Enjoy

THE WISH FACTORY
by Chris Riddell

"This glorious picture book, with its fantastic, highly imaginative illustrations, has a special purpose: to drive away big bad dreams." *Practical Parenting*

0-7445-6078-0   £4.99

BEN AND THE BEAR
by Chris Riddell

"One of my favourite 'Bear' books…
Good clear sentences suitable for children who have just started the reading habit or like a story read to them."
Belfast Telegraph

0-7445-5271-0   £4.99

QUACKY QUACK-QUACK
by Ian Whybrow / illustrated by Russell Ayto

This little baby had some bread; his mummy gave it to him for the ducks, but he started eating it instead…

And then the real rumpus began!

"A model of its kind… As whacky as it is quacky." *Brian Alderson, The Times*

"Children cannot help but join in." *Jill Bennett, School Librarian*

0-7445-3037-7   £4.99